T0193546

The Miraculous Clouds

Written by
Bob Morris

Illustrated by
Kim Merritt

Inspiring Voices books may be ordered through booksellers or by contacting:

Inspiring Voices
1663 Liberty Drive
Bloomington, IN 47403
www.inspiringvoices.com
1 (866) 697-5313

ISBN: 978-1-4624-1171-9 (sc)
ISBN: 978-1-4624-1172-6 (e)

Print information available on the last page.

Inspiring Voices rev. date: 5/10/2016

InspiringVoices

FOR GOD AND FAMILY

IT WAS ANOTHER BEAUTIFUL DAY IN CLAREMONT. THE SUN WAS SHINING, THE SKIES WERE BLUE, PEOPLE WERE SHOPPING IN THE VILLAGE, AND CHILDREN WERE PLAYING. NO ONE THOUGHT THE NEXT DAY WOULD BE SO DIFFERENT.

THAT NIGHT CLOUDS THAT SPARKLED WITH COLORS
ROLLED IN AND COMPLETELY COVERED THE VILLAGE.
ONLY PART OF A CHURCH STEEPLE APPEARED ABOVE
THE CLOUDS IN A SKY FILLED WITH BRIGHT STARS.
NO ONE HAD SEEN CLOUDS LIKE THESE BEFORE.

WHEN THE PEOPLE AWOKE THE NEXT MORNING, EVERYTHING IN THE VILLAGE HAD CHANGED COLORS. THE LEAVES ON A TREE WERE PURPLE. THE GRASS WAS NOT GREEN, BUT A CAT UNDER A TREE WAS. PEOPLE HAD CHANGED COLORS TOO.

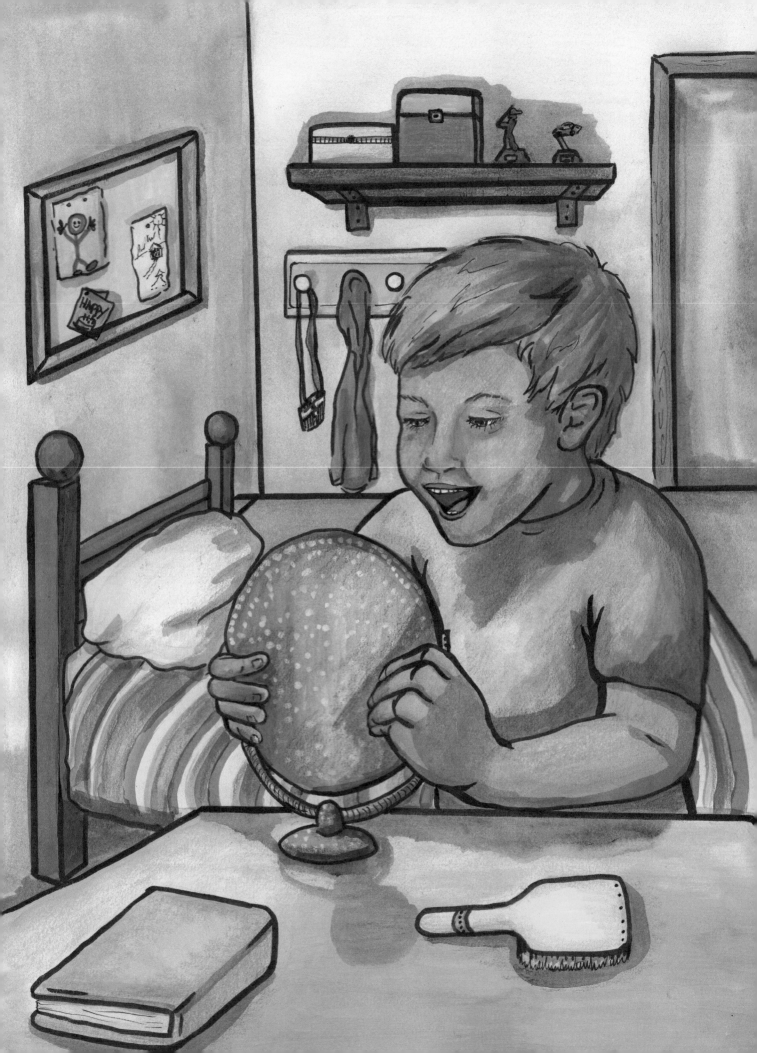

WHEN A BOY LOOKED IN A MIRROR, HE COULD NOT BELIEVE HIS EYES. HIS SKIN WAS ORANGE, AND HIS HAIR HAD TURNED BLUE.

BREAKFAST BANANAS TASTED THE SAME BUT LOOKED VERY DIFFERENT AND SO DID A GLASS OF MILK. ALTHOUGH PANCAKES WERE RED, THEY WERE STILL DELICIOUS. CHILDREN LIKED THE NEW COLORS.

A GIRL'S BROWN HORSE WAS NOW BLUE WITH A SILVER MANE AND TAIL, AND HER IRISH SETTER DOG WAS PINK. THE GIRL HAD CHANGED COLORS TOO.

AT THE PARK PLAYGROUND, CHILDREN WERE DIFFERENT COLORS. THE SWINGS AND SLIDE HAD CHANGED COLORS, AS HAD EVERYTHING ELSE. THE NOW GOLD CHAINS ON THE SWINGS WERE BEAUTIFUL. CHILDREN PLAYED HAPPILY TOGETHER LIKE THEY USUALLY DID. COLOR CHANGES MADE NO DIFFERENCE TO THEM.

COLORS HAD CHANGED AT THE VILLAGE LAKE TOO. CANADA GEESE DID NOT LOOK THE SAME, AND BRIGHTLY COLORED DUCKS SWAM ON WHAT USED TO BE BLUE WATER.

THE BARNYARD ON A FARM NEAR THE VILLAGE WAS AN AMAZING SIGHT. THE BARN WAS ORANGE, AND ALL OF THE ANIMALS HAD CHANGED COLORS. THEY DID NOT SEEM TO MIND AS THE COW MUNCHED ITS HAY, THE CHICKENS PECKED AT THE FEED, AND THE PIG GOBBLED HIS FOOD.

ANOTHER CHANGE FOR THE VILLAGE WAS COMING. ONE NIGHT WHITE CLOUDS WERE SO DENSE THAT PEOPLE COULD BARELY SEE THEIR HANDS IN FRONT OF THEIR FACES. A MOON SHOWN ABOVE, AND ITS GLITTERING MOONBEAMS COULD BE SEEN PASSING THROUGH THE WHITE CLOUDS..

THE NEXT DAY THE COLORS IN THE VILLAGE WERE CHANGED TO THE WAY THEY WERE SUPPOSED TO BE. THE PEOPLE WOULD NEVER FORGET THOSE FEW DAYS WHEN ALL COLORS HAD CHANGED. WHAT THEY REMEMBERED MOST WAS HOW EVERYONE LOOKED ON THE OUTSIDE WAS NOT IMPORTANT. THEY COULD BE TALL, SHORT, BIG, SMALL, OLD, YOUNG OR ANY COLOR. ALL THAT MATTERED WAS WHAT PEOPLE WERE LIKE ON THE INSIDE.

Printed in the United States
by Baker & Taylor Publisher Services